This Little Tiger book belongs to:

Liz Pichon (Lea shore) English writer

To Ella
who is a beautiful

butterfly

LITTLE TIGER PRESS
An imprint of Magi Publications
1 The Coda Centre, 189 Munster Road,
London SW6 6AW
www.littletigerpress.com

First published in Great Britain 2004
This edition published 2004
Text and illustrations copyright © Liz Pichon 2004
Liz Pichon has asserted her right to be identified
as the author and illustrator of this work under the
Copyright, Designs and Patents Act, 1988

The Very Ugly Bug

Liz Pichon

Little Tiger Press
London

There once was
an ugly bug.
A **very** ugly bug. _____ is it corona

no cos you can't

see corona ...

... but you can just

about see

bugs

She had **HUGE** big boggly eyes,

a really odd, wibbly wobbly-shaped head,

a horrible hairy back,

and wonky purple legs.

What a sight she was!

The very ugly bug
wondered why the other bugs
didn't look like her. So she asked them.
  "Spotty red bug, why are your eyes
so teeny tiny and not big and boggly
like mine?"
  "My eyes are teeny tiny so I can
hide in the berries and be safe from
birds," said the spotty red bug.

"Skinny green bug, why is your back
so smooth and green and not hairy
like mine?" asked the very ugly bug.
 "My smooth green back means
I can hide in the leaves and be safe
from birds," said the skinny
green bug.

"Shiny blue bug, why have you got such big fluttery wings, when I don't have any at all?" asked the very ugly bug.

"I use my big fluttery wings to fly away from birds, high up in the sky . . .

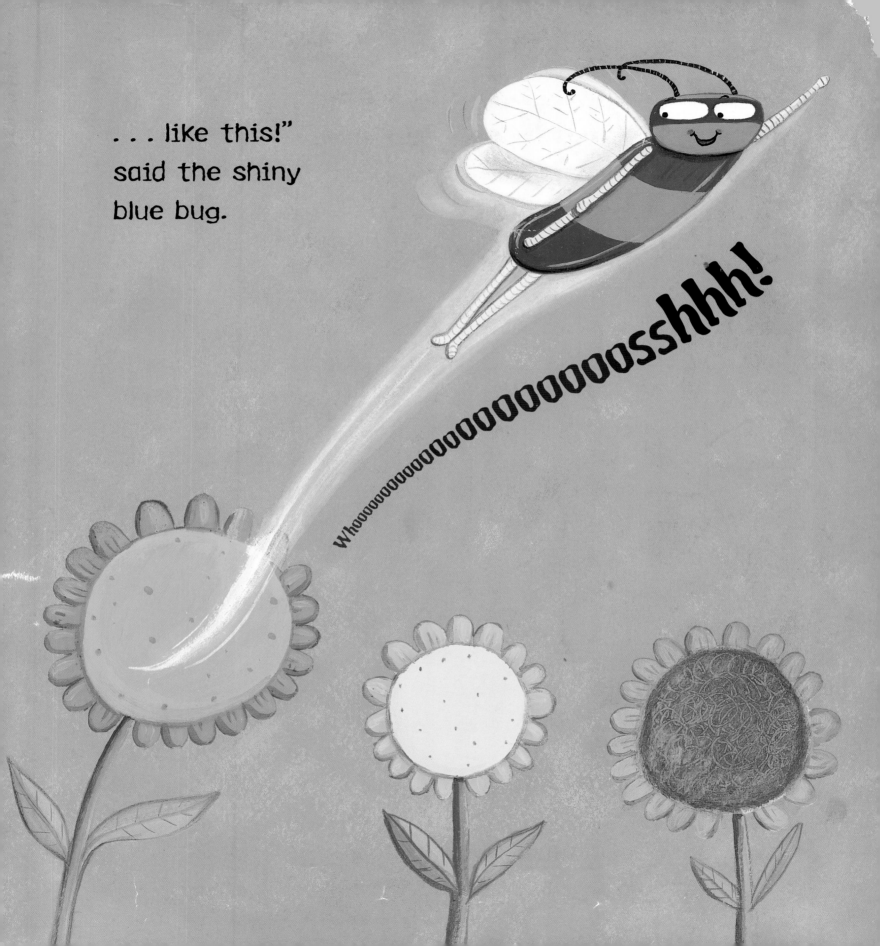

". . . like this!"
said the shiny
blue bug.

Whooooooooooooooooooosshhh!

"Hmmmm," thought the very ugly bug.

Nothing here!

"If only I had teeny tiny eyes, a smooth green back and

lovely fluttery wings then I would be safe from birds too!"

So the very ugly bug decided that she would make a mask to help her eyes look teeny tiny . . .

and use a leaf to make her back look smooth and green.

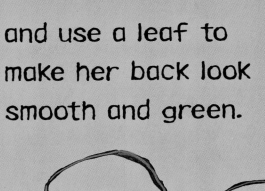

She even found a pair of fluttery wings. "I will be SO safe from birds now!" she said.

But she wasn't safe at all . . . The funny disguise made her stand out EVEN MORE! Now everyone could see her. Including a big hungry bird in the sky . . .

"Yum yum," said the bird. "Look at that lovely juicy bug down there. It looks delicious!" And he flew down for a tasty bug snack.

"ARGH!" screamed the very ugly bug as the bird swooped closer. The other bugs quickly hid and flew away. Then suddenly, something very strange began to happen . . .

The **BIG FRIGHT** made the very ugly bug get even uglier.

Her big boggly eyes got bigger.

Her odd-shaped head began to wibble and wobble.

Her horrible hairy back spiked up,

and her crooked purple legs waved in the air.

She looked HIDEOUS!

"**UGH!**" said the bird. "That bug looks **DISGUSTING.** It'll give me a tummy ache!" So he flew off to look for a nice juicy caterpillar instead.

"Hooray for the

very ugly bug!"

cheered the other bugs.
"She's SO ugly, she's scared
the bird away!"
"I love being ugly!" said
the very ugly bug proudly.
Mr Ugly Bug agreed.
He thought she
was gorgeous.

They fell madly in love and had
a huge family of baby bugs . . .

who were all even uglier
than they were!

Love Bugs

Get the reading bug, with books from Little Tiger Press!

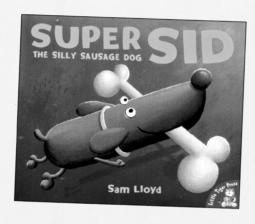

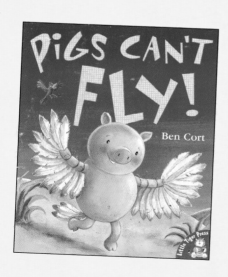

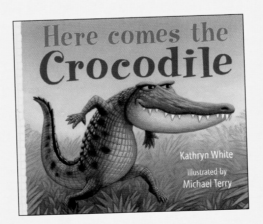

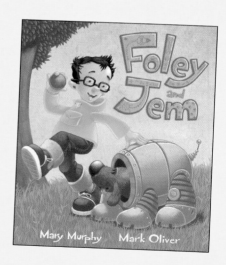

For information regarding any of the above titles or for our catalogue, please contact us:
Little Tiger Press, 1 The Coda Centre, 189 Munster Road, London SW6 6AW
Tel: 020 7385 6333 Fax: 020 7385 7333 Email: info@littletiger.co.uk
www.littletigerpress.com